THE ADVENTURES OF ROOBIE & RADLEY A

CHRISTMAS CAMPERVAN RESCUE

Catherine Brown

Published in 2018 by SilverWood Books

SilverWood Books Ltd
14 Small Street, Bristol, BS1 1DE, United Kingdom
www.silverwoodbooks.co.uk

ISBN 978-1-78132-825-5 (paperback)
ISBN 978-1-78132-826-2 (hardback)

British Library Cataloguing in Publication Data
A CIP catalogue record for this book is available from the British Library

Page design and typesetting by SilverWood Books

Printed on responsibly sourced paper

In loving memory of my mum Jean who taught me everything I know about strength, courage and determination.

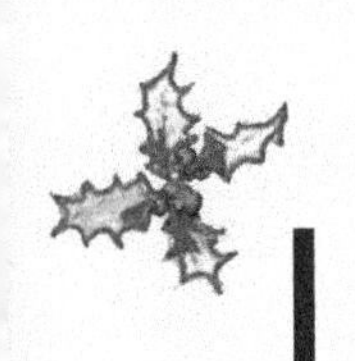

1 The Bones Bakery, Westie Green

'**Oooh**, it's so cold this morning,' said Roobie to her little brother Radley, as they walked along the snowy lane, back down towards **WESTIE GREEN.** Snowflakes continued to fall, landing on the end of their noses and whiskers.

'How many more **SLEEPS** is it to Christmas?' asked Radley.

'**TWELVE,**' replied Roobie.

'Oh, bother, that's a lot more than I thought!' said Radley.

'Twelve more windows to open on our **ADVENT CALENDAR**,' said Roobie.

'I do so like opening the windows,' said Radley.

'That's only because there are **BISCUITS** behind each window,' said Roobie, laughing.

'Yes, I had a turkey and cranberry one yesterday. It was **YUMMYTASTIC**. I'm hoping it's a cheese and pineapple one today,' said Radley.

'Oh, no you don't. Nice try: it's my **TURN** today!' cried Roobie.

'Come on, slowcoach – we've got to finish these deliveries before our noses drop off from the cold. I can't feel my paws anymore, and if my **TAIL** was a **WINDSCREEN** wiper, it would have snapped off by now!' said Roobie.

'Aye, I don't dare wag mine anymore. I'm not sure if I am **EVER** going to be able to wag it again!' said Radley, laughing out loud.

'We should have worn our **WELLINGTONS** – our feet would have stayed dry!' grunted Disco.

'AARGH, NO!' Radley suddenly shouted, his ears becoming more pointed as he spoke.

'HEY, you frightened me then. What's the matter?' Roobie said, looking at him, puzzled.

Disco, **FROZEN** to the spot, looked like he'd seen a ghost.

Radley moved his eyes from side to side several times, so the whites of his deep brown eyes could be seen. A wide **SMILE** crept onto his face.

'OH, I'm sorry,' he said, trying hard not to laugh because of the look of fear he had already put on their faces.

He moved forward towards their small delivery wagon and lifted up the red padded cushion in the bottom, pulling out **THREE** slightly crumpled, cream-coloured letters with stamps. Each of them was addressed:

For the attention of
SANTA CLAUS
North Pole
LAPLAND

'PHEW! I nearly forgot to post these,' he said, marching towards the red pillar box, clutching the letters in his paw. However, unable to quite reach the opening, Disco leapt forward and allowed Radley to **JUMP** up onto his back. They heard a **PLOP** as the letters dropped down into the box.

'AWESOME! Santa will get them in plenty of time now,' said Radley, feeling pleased as he jumped back down.

Their little **FEET** crunched loudly beneath them, as they continued to make their way along the winding lane for the last deliveries on their way home. Behind them, they left a trail of two sets of **PAWPRINTS** each, and a further set of four footprints – or, should we say, trotter prints, left by **Disco**, their **PET** piglet – in the freshly laid snow.

Disco had come to live with them after he was **RESCUED** by their mother and father. The local farmer, **Mr. Billy McGruff,** a rather grumpy, black Scottie dog, had decided that because Disco had failed to grow like the rest of the **PIGLETS** he had been born with, he was never going to get any bigger.

Because he was small, he also kept escaping under the fence into Westie Green or the **Westie Woods.**

Roobie and Radley had been delighted of course when the little **PIGLET** had come to live with them. The piglet followed them everywhere, usually walking or **TROTTING** a few paces behind them.

He got his name because every time he heard any **MUSIC** playing he started dancing – at first, he started **MOVING** to the beat using all four of his trotters. But he learned quickly and began to stand on just his back trotters, so he could wave his front trotters from side to side in time to the music. His **FAVOURITE** style of music turned out to be **DISCO!** Roobie and Radley **LOVED** that they had a dancing piglet for a pet.

Roobie and Radley lived in Westie Green with their mother and father at the **BROWN'S** family bakery, **THE BONES BAKERY.**

Westie Green is nestled deep in the West Highlands of Scotland and made up of mainly West Highland white terrier dogs. They are often called Westies for short. A few black Scottie dogs had also come to join them.

All the buildings and houses they had built themselves and were wooden huts. Their little community was known locally, and they were often called the Westie Green Hutters.

The Bones Bakery made **TARTAN BONES**: gravy-flavoured bone-shaped biscuits, which were handmade with paws of love…

This Christmas they had a new flavour: TURKEY and **CRANBERRY.** These were proving popular, both for eating during the festive season, and were also selling fast as

Christmas **GIFTS.** There was also a vegetarian flavour especially for Christmas, which was cheese and **cranberry.**

Other **FLAVOURS** that they did all year round included cheese and pineapple, Aberdeen Angus Beef with Tatties **(potatoes)**, Scottish Salmon and Cream Cheese with **CHIVES.**

The bakery made all types of breads, cakes and gingerbread biscuits which were in the shape of ducks, **FROGS** and other woodland animals. These had icing on top with little decorations to highlight their features, like **CURRANTS** for eyes, and little jellies for noses and mouths. These were extremely popular with the younger Westie Hutters and always **SOLD OUT.**

There were delicious doughnuts, which had the most unusual and **SCRUMMYTASTIC (in the words of Radley)** centres.

Sergeant Brown was Roobie and Radley's Auntie and she called in daily to collect a bag of her favourite toffee apple-flavoured ones. As she was their father's sister, she was sometimes given an **EXTRA** doughnut or two!

She was the local officer for Westie Green and had been so for years. **(Her uniform had expanded over this time, and this was perhaps from eating far too many doughnuts!)**

They sold an assortment of flavours of **CUPCAKES** that were displayed in neat little rows on trays on top of the wooden counter. There were bright yellow **DUCKS** with pineapple icing, sitting on pale blue buttercream made to look like water and tasting of blueberries. There were lime green **crocodiles** that tasted of spearmint, sitting on swampy-looking chocolate butter cream – when your teeth sank down through the crocodile's long mouth, an unusual-tasting sour apple jelly **SQUISHED** out and ran down your chin!

As Christmas drew nearer, **snowmen, Santas, and reindeer** were added daily. Sometimes, when all the ovens were on and it was very hot, Santa's beard melted and ran down over the cupcake case – this made him look more like a long-bearded **GARDEN GNOME!** They still tasted scrummytastic, because Radley said that they were!

Lots of pale, wispy grey smoke could be seen drifting into the cold winter's air from their busy little ovens. The most delicious smells also wafted through Westie Green. Many of the Westie Green Hutters' **BIG** black noses sniffed into the air daily and tried hard to **IDENTIFY** what was being baked. This was good for business, as it made them come into the bakery just to see if they had guessed **RIGHT!**

Most of their deliveries they did in **DAISY,** a purple and white **VW Campervan** belonging to Grandpa Angus, which was almost as old as he was. Daisy was the same colour as the wooden hut of the bakery and the spare wheel on the front had a **BIG** pair of crossed bones on it. This was the same **LOGO** that they also used on all their boxes at the bakery.

At busy times such as **CHRISTMAS,** Roobie and Radley used their wagon to help

Grandpa Angus out with some of the local deliveries.

Next to the bakery was an **ENORMOUS** oak tree. At the bottom of the tree trunk was a **MASSIVE** archway, which went right through the middle of the tree. You could drive in one side and back out the other. Grandpa Angus parked Daisy in there, using the tree as a **GARAGE.**

Grandpa Angus remembered the tree always being there and told Roobie and Radley it was called the **Wise Westie Tree of Wisdom.**

Some Westie Green Hutters said you could see the **LARGE** face of a West Highland Terrier on the trunk if you stared at it hard and for long enough, and the tree was believed to have **MAGICAL POWERS.**

Roobie and Radley had stared hard at the **TRUNK** many times, but when Grandpa Angus asked if they had seen the face, only Radley had said he could. Ever since that day, the tree had been renamed

THE

TREE

OF

AWE-

SOME-

NESS,

because as Radley had said, that was what it was!

2 Westie Green Loch And Hidden Treasure

Roobie and Radley stood in the **DELIVERY** area of the bakery and finished loading up their wagon. It was full up with boxes of **Tartan Bones** biscuits of every flavour. This was going to make pulling it in the snow extra hard – work not helped by Disco, who was sat on **TOP** of the boxes.
They were keen to get their biscuits delivered quickly today, so they could visit Grandpa Angus and Grandma Soozie's house. They lived at the far end of **Westie Green Loch.**

They loved going to visit because Grandpa Angus always had so many cool things that he collected and recycled. He also **INVENTED** things. In the summer, he had made an outdoor hot tub from an old skip that had been discarded on the edge of **Westie Woods**. Radley loved this as it had hot water with jets that made big foamy bubbles if you pressed a button. Grandpa Angus had collected old bicycle wheels, which he had found in the Loch when **FISHING.** From these he had made solar powered panels which heated the water.

Grandpa Angus was a keen artist, and always wore an artist's **BLACK BERET.** He rarely took it off, not even when he was in bed. Grandma Soozie said she thought he kept **SNACKS** underneath it, because it was often covered in crumbs!

It had been a gift from his French cousin **Basile Bourbon** when he came to visit whilst on his summer holidays. Basile belonged to a large Westie Hutter community who lived in a woodland in **FRANCE.**

Grandpa Angus told Roobie and Radley that there were probably other communities of Westie Hutters living all over the **WORLD,** but Basile was the only one that he'd met so far.

'What time are we meeting Grandma Soozie?' asked Radley.

'We have to meet her in **Woolly Ball's** at lunchtime: she has some wool to collect from there,' replied Roobie.

'Oh, I love it in that shop,' said Radley.

This was where Grandma Soozie got all her **WOOL** for her knitting. Mrs. McLean, the owner, mostly used fleeces supplied by Farmer McGruff's **HIGHLAND SHEEP,** which she spun and dyed herself. It was a great shop that was one half wool and the other half toys, gifts and household **ITEMS.**

Radley had heard Grandma Soozie say, **'it stocked everything from a pin to an elephant**,' but he had never seen an elephant in there, despite him looking every time he went in!

Lunchtime came, and they met in the shop. There were **Christmas lights** in both front windows of the painted pink wooden hut, and lights on the shelves inside.

Mrs. McLean always dressed in the colour pink – she even had pink shoes and glasses. She loved **FLUFFY** jumpers and today she had a dark pink one on. Radley had told Roobie that she was the **FLUFFYTASTIC** lady, which was a cross between fluffy and fantastic **(Radley often made these types of words up).**

Roobie and Radley looked around the shop and spotted some small knitted teddies, including a bright red and green one that they really liked the look of, whilst Disco **BOUNCED** up and down like he was on a trampoline on some odd balls of wool that were in a basket near the door.

Grandma Soozie told him off, but Mrs. Fluffytastic McLean said he was fine, which just made him **BOUNCE** even higher!

They paid for the wool, which was to finish off some Christmas jumpers that Grandma Soozie had knitted for **PRESENTS.** They walked down through Westie Green and along the edge of the woods, down to **Westie Green LOCH.** Tied to a large tree was a small purple wooden rowing boat.

Grandpa Angus and Grandma Soozie's house could only be reached by boat and this was the reason Daisy the campervan was kept at the **Bones Bakery**.

Although Roobie and Radley could both row the little boat, their mother and father had told them that they **MUST** always have an adult with them.

There was a lot of snow around the tree as Roobie untied the rope of the boat. The edges of the Loch were frozen.

'WOWZERS, they look like **SHARKS!'** shouted Radley, as he looked at the broken-up pieces of ice that were now floating all around them from where they had slid the boat into the water.

Radley loved reading about sharks and he had a blue rubber one he took into the bath with him, which shot water out of its **MOUTH**.

'OOOH, you scared me then, Radley.' Grandma Soozie looked lovingly at him as she laughed out loud.

'You'll be saying that you can see the **Loch Ness Monster** next,' said Roobie, also laughing.

Grandpa Angus had once told Radley that there were **crocodiles** in the Loch **(which there aren't).** After this, Radley spent such a long time looking for them and was so disappointed because he hadn't found any that Grandpa Angus felt guilty and **BOUGHT** them each a big crocodile-shaped bed to sleep in.

They kept to the **MIDDLE** of the Loch to avoid the ice and rowed the short distance. Grandma Soozie sat at one end of the **BOAT** and Disco at the other, with Roobie and Radley in the middle with the oars.

Grandpa Angus was standing waiting for them by the wooden **JETTY** and helped them tie the boat up. They made their way up to the house, a brightly coloured wooden **HUT** that he had made from recycling old pallets.

Grandma Soozie made some hot chocolate with gingerbread bone biscuits and they sat huddled together by the **CRACKLING** fire to warm themselves back up.

'Come here – I have a present for you,' said Grandma Soozie, handing them each a neatly wrapped parcel, tied up with a large red bow and a **GIFT TAG** with their names on.

'AWESOME, and it's not even Christmas yet,' said Radley excitedly.

Disco was already standing on top of his parcel making pleased **GRUNTING** noises, ready to use all four trotters in an attempt to rip open his first. But before he could, he heard—

'Ready, on the count of three. **ONE…TWO…THREE,**' shouted out Grandma Soozie.

The room filled with the sound of tearing and **RUSTLING** as the Christmas paper was torn and ripped off their parcels.

Roobie, with a big grin on her face, was holding up a ruby red sweater, Radley a bright green one, both with a picture of a **BIG** brown reindeer on the front. Disco had a red and green **STRIPED** one similar to the one he was wearing. He only had the one sweater, which he managed to get a lot of stains on!

Disco made loud pleased **OINKING** noises as he wriggled around, trying to put his new sweater on without much success. He had put his head through the **ARM** hole rather than the head opening.

Roobie helped him put it on correctly, and then he began dancing around the room with delight. Radley joined in as well, whilst Grandma Soozie, who was **SITTING** in her rocking chair, started knitting again, and Roobie laughed at them.

'So glad you like them,' said Grandma Soozie, rocking gently in her chair.

'**Aye**, we don't like them – we **LOVE** them,' said Roobie.

Wearing their new **CHRISTMAS SWEATERS,** Grandma Soozie found aprons and a tea towel, which she tied around Disco to keep them clean. They helped stir the

Christmas pudding mix which smelled deliciously **FRUITY.** They were each allowed to taste the mixture by licking the wooden spoon, add a silver coin and make a wish before Grandma Soozie **ADDED** some Scottish whisky and brandy.

'What if someone **SWALLOWS** the coin?' asked Radley, who had brown pudding mixture all around his whiskers and on both of his paws.

'You have to eat your pudding slowly, so that you can check with your spoon for coins. It's like looking for **HIDDEN** treasure in your dish,' Grandma Soozie told him.

Radley thought to himself on hearing this. He always ate his food fast, because he was always hungry, **BUT** he would definitely be slowly checking for hidden treasure in his pudding dish on Christmas day. He **COULDN'T** wait.

They joined Grandpa Angus in his shed. He had both snowy paws and boots. He had been busy **HOWKING (digging)** up some tatties **(potatoes)**, from the frozen ground. He had ready a sack of neeps (swedes) and tatties that he was going to put in the boat to take back to Westie

Green for **The Green Shed.** This was a shop, a green wooden hut that looked just like a **SHED,** where Westie Hutters could buy all their vegetables. All the vegetables that Grandpa Angus grew were **ORGANIC.**

They spent the rest of the afternoon sticking **PAPER CHAINS** together whilst listening and singing to Christmas music from Grandpa Angus's solar powered radio. They managed to make **ENOUGH** for their bedroom and the Bones Bakery.

'This is one of my favourite things about Christmas,' said Roobie as Radley and Disco helped pack the shiny red and green coloured chains into a wicker basket. They were made from **OFFCUTS** of Christmas wrapping paper and so had cost nothing to make.

Grandpa Angus took the little trio back to Westie Green in the boat.

They had one more job for the day to do on their way home, and that was to drop off the vegetables to Farmer McGruff at **The Green Shed.** This was unfortunately at the top of the hill. Farmer McGruff was quite pleased to see them today, for a change. However, this changed quickly when Disco entered the shed and started **EATING** some carrots from a box he found on the counter.

Roobie decided it was time to leave, and **QUICKLY** put Disco into their cart. There wasn't enough room for Radley as they had some vegetables for their mother. So, Radley grabbed two nearby sprout stalks that he decided would make the most perfect ski poles to get away as fast as he could!

'**GOODBYE** Mr. McGruff,' shouted Radley as he wobbled off down the hill in the snow, waving one sprout stalk each side of him. As Radley **WHOOSHED** off down to the bottom of the hill, and finally landed in a **HEAP** at the bottom, he told Roobie and Disco that he didn't quite hear what Mr. McGruff had shouted out to him. He had, but he wasn't going tell them what he had said!

On the plus side, his mother was **DELIGHTED** with him that she had some extra sprouts for the Westie Green Christmas dinner and he got an extra **BIG** portion of Scottish Beef Stew for his dinner.

They all went to bed early, as the next day they had an **IMPORTANT** meeting with someone that none of them wanted to miss!

3 The Polar Bear And The Santa Train

Roobie and Radley were awake extra early. They were super **EXCITED** this morning, as they were off on an adventure to see **SANTA**, and they would be going by **STEAM TRAIN!**

Disco was sitting on the window ledge. He was drawing patterns with his trotters on the window pane, which had **FROSTED** up with ice from the cold overnight.

'It's still snowing and we're off to see Santa,' squealed Disco with **DELIGHT.**

Radley yawned and stretched out his legs in his bright green **CROCODILE** shaped bed. They all had one which kept them snuggly and warm all night, as it got very cold in winter at Westie Green.

Roobie chuckled to herself whilst watching Disco trying his best to **DRAW** a Santa face, without much success!

Disco was wearing a bright purple **ONESIE** with little silver stars all over it. He stood up onto his back trotters, and started spinning around on the spot several times, like a ballerina. He **WOBBLED** quite a bit whilst doing this. It was hard to get a grip on the window ledge whilst his **TROTTERS** were covered up inside his onesie.

He started to slip and slide around, and he began singing the **'Good morning'** song, the song they always sung together every morning when they woke up.

He sang;

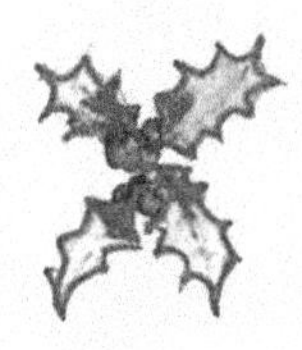

Good morning, good morning, good morning to you!
Good morning, good morning Master Radley, good morning to you!
Good morning, good morning Roobie Roo, good morning to you!

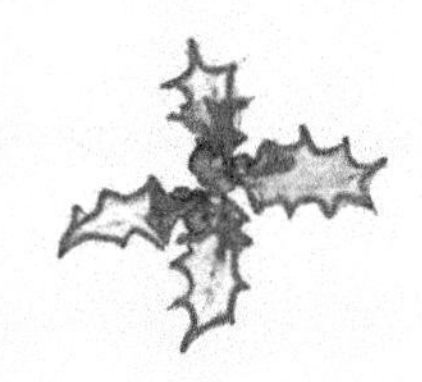

Roobie and Radley joined in with the singing, each wishing each other a good morning. However, Disco got a bit carried away with **BOTH** singing and dancing and **SLIPPED** on some of the ice he had scraped from the window. He flipped himself backwards off the ledge, did two backward rolls mid-air and landed back into his crocodile bed with just his **HEAD** poking out. He began squealing with laughter.

'That will teach you,' said Roobie, roaring with laughter.

'That was totally **AWESOME,**' Radley said, with tears running down his face.

They then heard their mother shout, 'Come on, you **SCALLYWAGS,** time for breakfast!'

'What **TIME** are we leaving to catch the train?' asked Radley as he eagerly ate his big bowl of Scottish **PORRIDGE** oats.

'Grandpa Angus and Grandma Soozie are collecting you at 10.30,' replied his mother.

'And Radley, don't speak with your **MOUTH FULL!**' cried his mother.

'**SORRY,**' he replied in a muffled tone with his mouth still full of porridge.

Roobie tried not to laugh out loud at him, so continued making a face in her dish using blueberries as eyes and a mouth and a **BIG** strawberry for a nose.

'Roobie, **DON'T** play around with your food!' shouted her mother.

Radley scrunched his little face up, shutting his eyes as he did this. He was **SMILING** to himself because Roobie had been told off. He did **LOVE** his big sister, but she was such a good girl. She rarely got told off or got into any trouble. Not like him, he thought. He was a **RASCAL.** His mother often called him that, whatever one of those was!

Disco was sitting under the kitchen table waiting for any **CRUMBS** which might fall his way when the toast was ready. Although he was part of the family, he wasn't allowed to sit at the table with them at mealtimes as he was their **PET.** He wasn't **ALLOWED** to have porridge either, because the last time he did, he had stood in the **DISH** with his trotters, and then tipped it up, and had managed to mash it all over the floor. It had been like a **STICKY GLUE** which had taken their mother ages to clean up.

Most mornings he had warm mashed **POTATO** peelings, with carrots and any other leftover vegetables, which was a much cleaner option! Sometimes Radley put a couple of stale cakes or doughnuts leftover from the Bakery into his mix when he thought **NOBODY** was looking!

Disco wasn't supposed to have too much sugar, and neither were Radley or Roobie. Mrs. Dalzell, their school teacher, said it was bad for your **TEETH** and eating too much of it could make you **FAT!** When they asked their father if this was true, he said that if they cleaned their teeth properly twice a day and only ate sugary things **NOW** and again, this was O.K.

On the **DOT** of 10.30, Grandpa Angus and Grandma Soozie arrived at the bakery to collect the little trio, who were standing eagerly awaiting their arrival. It had been snowing again all night, and there was an even **THICKER** blanket of snow on the ground.

Westie Green had very few vehicles – nobody really needed to go anywhere, and nobody really **WANTED** to go anywhere. But today the little trio were going to see Santa, and if this meant leaving Westie Green for a few **HOURS,** then today this is what they desperately wanted to do!

The Santa train was going to collect them from **WESTIE GREEN RAILWAY STATION.** To get there, they had to walk down through Westie Woods, and then climb through a gap in the **HEDGE**. This led them down a small narrow footpath, which ran along the canal path and then up to the railway station.

Westie Green railway station had been decorated for Christmas. There were **HOLLY WREATHS** with big red bows around the lamp posts, and coloured Christmas lights around the roof and window of the brick-built ticket office.

Grandpa Angus went into the ticket office and bought tickets for the journey and a copy of **The Westie Times** newspaper. He stayed in the waiting room with Grandma Soozie, as he said it was too cold to stand waiting.

Roobie, Radley, and Disco were too excited to wait in the waiting room, so went out to wait for the Santa train on the station platform. They joined the guard, **Mr. Dalzell,** who was wearing a cap and dressed in his smart navy-blue jacket and tartan trousers. He had a green and red flag in his **PAWS.**

'Would you like to wave the **RED FLAG** to stop the train when we see it coming, Master Radley?' said Mr. Dalzell.

'OOOH, yes please!' excitedly replied Radley.

Mr. Dalzell handed Radley the **RED FLAG** which was on a wooden pole and showed him how he had to wave it.

They didn't have to wait long: they could **HEAR** the train as it approached and see the **BIG** white clouds of smoke coming from the steam train's engine. Driving the train was **Mr. RUFUS THE BEAR,** as he was known to his friends. He was a large, extremely fluffy Westie who looked just like a Polar Bear. He began waving to them from the driver's **WINDOW.**

As the train approached, Radley stepped forward and started waving the flag **FURIOUSLY** up and down. Disco danced up and down on the spot with excitement and in doing so nearly lost his wellingtons.

Roobie shouted out for Grandpa Angus and Grandma Soozie to come and join them, but they were already on the platform, having heard the **TRAIN.**

Mr. Dalzell praised Radley for his **EXCELLENT** flag-waving skills, and he opened the doors to their carriage for them. They all clambered in and the train began to pull away **SLOWLY** along the track.

Grandma Soozie ordered lunch for them and the **WAITER** brought, on a fancy plate, some delicious turkey sandwiches, sausage rolls, mince pies, round **BUNS** with icing which had a big cherry on the top. They also had glass bottles of homemade lemonade with a paper straw.

They **MUNCHED** their lunch whilst looking out the window as they chugged along in the old steam carriage, passing through the snowy-topped, purple mountains that surrounded Westie Green.

There were lots of sounds of **CLICK-a-de CLACK, CLICKERLY CLACK** over and over as the wheels sang over the railway track. As the train neared the Santa station platform, the train made the sound **Aar Ooooo, Aar Ooooo.** Then, just before they pulled in at the stop, there was a **Choo-Choo, Woo, Woooooo, Woo,** and

then finally a loud **Ding-Dang, Ding-Dong** as Mr. Dalzell rang the big brass bell.

There were big clouds of white smoke as the train stood still, which filled up the whole of the platform. Mr. Dalzell opened the doors of the train, and they scrambled out onto a tiny snowy-filled **PLATFORM.** They could just about see through the smoke and make out a sleigh with four dark brown, furry **REINDEER** attached to it.

There was an Elf called **BUDDY** who was holding onto a set of shiny red leather reins. The elf looked at them and smiled and said, **'ALL ABOARD** those who are going **ABOARD**! Next stop, **SANTA!'**

4 Santa And The Ice Cave

The **SLEIGH** set off and slid smoothly over the snow, pulled by four **BIG** brown furry reindeer. They had names in gold lettering on each of their red leather headbands, which read **PRANCER, DASHER, DANCER** and **CUPID.**

After what seemed a far too short but enjoyable journey riding in the sleigh, they stopped outside an enormous **ICE CAVE.**

The outside was covered with tiny icicle sparkling lights which hung down and **TWINKLED** blue, pink and silver colours. At the entrance to the cave, a warm golden light shone out and there were brightly coloured fairy lights.

The Elf said, **'Follow me!'**

Grandpa Angus and Grandma Soozie waited at the entrance and let the trio follow the **ELF.**

Once inside, there was the most delightful and **DELICIOUS** smell, a mixture of mince pies, gingerbread biscuits, and sweet candy canes. There was an enormous Christmas tree which smelt of fresh **PINE**, like the smell of the trees that were in the Westie Green Woods.

HUNG on the Christmas tree were hundreds of twinkling fairy lights as well as the most Christmas decorations dangling down that they had ever seen. Christmas music was playing **SOFTLY** in the background and the Elf suddenly **STOPPED** and said, 'Santa, you have some visitors.' The Elf disappeared then, and they could see that sitting in front of them in a big dark green **VELVET** armchair was Santa.

Santa peered over his small round glasses, which were perched on the end of his nose. He smiled, and in a deep and jolly voice said, **'Ho, Ho, Ho, MERRY CHRISTMAS, Roobie, Radley and Disco.'**

'How do you know our names, Santa?' asked Radley.

Santa chuckled out loud, and replied, 'I am Santa, and I know everyone's name.'

'Wow, that's AWESOME!' said Radley.

Santa reached down by the side of his chair and pulled out a really old-looking brown leather satchel, which had red and green stitching. On the front, it said **'LETTERS'**.

Santa pulled out three letters on cream paper which they recognised as the ones that they had **written** to him.

'I have looked through your letters, and as I say to all the children I see, I **CANNOT** promise to bring anything or everything you have asked for from your list. But I will do my best, and make sure that you get something from me for Christmas,' said **SANTA.**

'Oh, let me check first – I nearly forgot, silly me – are you on the **NAUGHTY** or **NICE** list?' said Santa, chuckling loudly.

They watched Santa pulled out a **LONG LIST** from his letters satchel bag and began checking through this.

Radley stared at Santa's face, his eyes not moving, and waited nervously. He knew that Roobie Roo and Disco would be both on the **NICE** list, but he couldn't be certain that he was **NOT** on the **NAUGHTY** list. He was, as his mother told him often, a bit of a rascal!

After what seemed like a really long wait, Santa looked directly at Radley and smiled.

'You will be pleased to know you're **ALL** on my **NICE** list!'

'**PHEW,** thank you Santa,' said Radley, letting out a **SIGH** of relief.

'Now, just before you go, I have a small present for you each to be going on with, until I visit you of course on Christmas Eve,' said Santa.

Santa reached down into a large **GREEN** sack which was tied round with a **BIG** red bow.

He handed Roobie and Radley two equally-sized wrapped Christmas parcels with **SHINY** red paper on.

Just as Disco began to think that Santa had forgotten about him, he heard Santa say, 'I have something **SPECIAL** for you, young Disco.'

They all **WATCHED** Santa as he reached in to his satchel again. Roobie thought to herself that Santa's satchel was the best **BAG** that she had ever seen. It was like a magician's hat that you could keep pulling surprises out of!

Santa pulled out a small red leather collar, which had a tiny silver bell attached.

'I had some spare leather left over from making the **REINDEER** new collars, and a **SPARE BELL,**' he said, reaching out to put the collar around Disco's neck.

As soon as Disco moved his head, the silver bell gave out a jingle.

'Oh, what a **SMARTY PANTS** you look!' said Roobie.

'Aye, that's pretty awesome,' said Radley.

Disco began letting out squeals of delight, in between lots of **NOISY** oinks, and threw himself up into the air.

'Aye, he loves it, Santa. Thank you,' said Radley, speaking for Disco.

'When he gets **EXCITED** he can't speak,' explained Roobie, laughing.

Santa smiled and joined in with the laughing.

'It **SUITS** you: just the right size!'

With that, Buddy, the Elf from earlier, came back into the cave and it was time for them to say **GOODBYE** to Santa. As they were leaving, Santa said, 'Roobie and Radley, I think you will find your gifts to be **MORE** useful than you might think. I just have a feeling that you **WILL!'**

On the way back out of the ice cave, they saw several of their friends queueing at the entrance. Miss Tilly Bean and Archy Turner and Popsie were there, and the McGruff brothers. They managed to **WAVE** briefly as the sleigh arrived to take them back to the train.

On the journey back to Westie Green Station, Roobie and Radley **RIPPED** opened their present from Santa. They each had a **TORCH** small enough to fit in the pocket of their coats.

Grandpa Angus was excited when he saw them, as when he looked at the instructions, he saw that they were **solar** with a dynamo and a wind-up fold away handle **(secretly he wished he had one of these and hoped that Santa might bring him one in his Christmas stocking).**

'You can use those when you are out on your **DELIVERIES,**' said Grandpa Angus, looking lovingly at the torches.

'Make sure you keep them in your pocket now, so that you have got them if you **NEED** them,' said Grandma Soozie, who was trying to see and talk over the top of Disco's head.

He was sitting on her lap but kept **jigging** about so that his bell around his neck made a **jingle.**

On the walk back to the Bones Bakery they saw their Auntie **POPPY** on her **RED** bicycle riding along the canal path. She lived on a narrowboat called **Poppy's Canal Side Café.** She was their mother's sister.

At this time of the year, the café was not so busy, and she often helped with deliveries from the bakery at Christmas – the bakery's busiest time of year.

She had a large **WICKER** basket on the front and back of her bike. Sometimes she would give Radley a ride in the front basket of her bike. If she wasn't too busy in the café she often made them hot frothy milk or hot chocolate with **MARSHMALLOWS** that floated on the top and gave them something to eat.

Radley and Disco didn't always let on that they had already had food at Poppy's café when they got home, as they were always **HUNGRY**. However, Roobie couldn't usually manage to eat her dinner back at home. Radley and Disco never had this **PROBLEM** and always managed two dinners!

Poppy gave Grandpa Angus and Grandma Soozie a **BIG** hug and did the same to Roobie and Radley. They were her **FAVOURITE** niece and nephew.

'Look forward to seeing you all at the **carol** concert on **Christmas Eve,**' she shouted as she stood on the canal path waving to them with both of her paws high in the **AIR.**

She watched them until they disappeared out of sight, as they walked back through the gap into the hedge towards **Westie Woods.**

5 The Tartan Frog Carol Concert

Every year the Westie Green Hutters held a **CHRISTMAS** Carol Concert at **The Tartan Frog.** The oldest West Highland terrier lived there and was known as **Sir Wesley.** Nobody really knew how old he was, but he had lived there for many, many, years. He had lots of **Westie Wisdom** which he was always keen to share with the youngest Hutters, or the bairns **(little ones)** as he called them.

The Tartan Frog was a **BRIGHT GREEN** wooden hut, which at the front had a large round stone pond with a frog. There was a metal pub sign hanging up, which had a picture of a frog wearing a tartan kilt dancing on it. If there were any **IMPORTANT** Hutter community matters, then this is where the Hutters met to discuss it.

The **ELDER** Hutters met up there most weeks for a **Wee Dram,** as they called it, or a bottle of Scottish broon **(brown)** beer in Sir Wesley's front room. Some of these same Hutters said they had in fact seen a frog dancing in a kilt near the **POND. (The truth of this remained a mystery!)**

There was always much **EXCITEMENT** about the carol concert and there were always lots of things to get ready. Sir Wesley owned a piano which he always asked Billy McGruff to help him move.

Farmer Billy McGruff always moaned about not having the time to move the '**BLOOMING**' piano, and that he hated '**BLOOMING**' Christmas!' But each year without fail he appeared when it was time to get it wheeled outside and was always the first one to start the carol singing off, which was amazing for someone who claimed he didn't like **CHRISTMAS!**

Mrs. Molly Dalzell, the wife of the train station guard, was the **school teacher** and she played the Christmas carols on the **PIANO.** This year she had asked if Disco could turn the sheet music for her. He had been **DELIGHTED** with this request and accepted straight away.

TARTAN
FROG
CAROLS
GWR

At last year's concert, some of the younger Hutters had been put off their singing by Disco's dancing. Mrs. Dalzell hoped by keeping him **BUSY** this year, that there wouldn't be any time for him to dance!

Roobie and Radley were going to be singing carols with their **family** and friends from school. Radley's **BEST PAL** Archy Turner and his little sister Popsie were helping his mother who had a **toffee apple** and popcorn cart. Radley and Archy were hoping they might get a **FREE** toffee apple. Sir Wesley had asked if Archy's mother could also serve hot **mulled wine** and mince pies.

It was Friday **24th** December: **CHRISTMAS EVE** and the day of the Christmas Carol Concert had finally arrived. It got dark early at Westie Green due to the location in the **HIGHLANDS** where they lived. Most of the Hutters had placed coloured Christmas lights around their huts and with the glittering, white snow the whole place looked **MAGICAL.**

Every Friday in Westie Green it was a **tradition** that all the Hutters gathered to queue up for a fish and chip supper. They called Fridays **Fishy Friday.**

Mr. Bruce McLean had a blue and cream painted wooden hut called **THE SALTY SEA DOG,** where he cooked and served freshly made fish and chips. The delicious smell of these cooking would drift around Westie Green and made the Hutters feel hungry. It was Roobie and Radley's favourite day of the week. They were all going to gather for a **FISH** supper after the Carol concert.

Sir Wesley stood at the front door of **The Tartan Frog.** He was wearing Highland dress with included his best **KILT.** He was handing out sheets with the Carols written on, so everybody knew the words.

Radley and Archy Turner often came up with their own words. Sir Wesley had heard

them singing **'NO SPROUTS, NO SPROUTS,'** to most of the Carols at last year's concert.

This year **BOTH** had been asked to carry outside Mrs. Dalzell's piano stool by Sir Wesley, but unbeknownst to him, Archy had already sprinkled itching powder on it!

Radley had also come up with the **IDEA** of placing his bath time rubber shark into the pond, and then they got Archy's little sister Popsie and their friend Miss Tilly Bean to tell the Winfield Westies that they had seen a **SHARK** in the pond.

The Winfield Westies were siblings **Harvey, Theo and Chloe.** They had looked into the pond and were **FRIGHTENED** when they saw a blue **shark fin** swimming about. So, they told Sergeant Brown who went to investigate. She **SOON** discovered what Radley and Archy had done and **SEIZED** the shark. She needed a plan to teach these two rascals a lesson.

At **4pm** everyone gathered, and the **CAROL SINGING** began. Disco felt very important sat on top of the piano turning the music pages for Mrs. Dalzell. Radley felt **PROUD** of Disco, as he managed not to do any dancing!

However, poor Mrs. Dalzell began to **MOVE** around on her Piano stool backwards and forwards and then side to side like she was at a **ROCK** concert. The longer she sat there, the more she began to **JIG** about. She kept letting out **'Oooh's,'** and **'Ahah's.'**

Her piano playing speeded up too, which made her get through the **CAROLS** much more quickly than normal.

She just couldn't understand why her tail and bottom felt so **ITCHY.** But what Radley and Archy didn't **REALISE** was that Sergeant Brown had already **SEEN** the pot of itching powder as it was sticking out of Archy Turner's trouser pocket.

After the last carol **'The Holly and the Ivy'** had been sung, Sir Wesley and Farmer McGruff took it in turns to play the bagpipes. The effects of the itching powder had **THANKFULLY** worn off, so Mr. and Mrs. Dalzell were able to join in with the **Scottish** Dancing with some of the other Westie Hutters.

Everybody was wishing each other a **HAPPY CHRISTMAS.** They would all meet up again on Christmas day for the Christmas dinner and candlelight party in **Westie Woods.**

Roobie, Radley and Disco joined the queue for their **FISHY FRIDAY** supper. Tonight, the queue was extra-long, so Mrs. Fluffytastic McLean was taking the orders and passing out the wrapped fish suppers. Radley heard someone say that the orders were **flying out,** but as hard as he stared at the **Salty Sea Dog** fish and chip hut, he didn't manage to see anything **FLYING!**

When they got **BACK** home with their supper they sat around the table to unwrap them. Their mother got some plates out and Radley was the last to unwrap his supper and what a surprise he got. Instead of his piece of crispy battered fish that he had been expecting, there in front of him staring back at him was a **BIG BLUE FIN.** It was only his rubber bath **SHARK!**

'Sergeant Brown said that this might teach you a lesson, Radley?' said father. Roobie couldn't stop laughing but neither could Radley – his **crime** had been discovered.

Roobie gave Radley some of her fish as she couldn't eat all of hers, which made him **INCREDIBLY** happy because as we know, he was always hungry.

It was still only **6pm** and Grandpa Angus had asked that Roobie and Radley meet him down in Westie Woods, to help him collect the Christmas tree needed for the Westie

Green **Christmas Day celebrations.**

Just before they left, they remembered to hang their **STOCKINGS** on the fireplace ready for Santa later. They each had a stocking with their name on it. Roobie hung them all up as she was the only one that could reach.

The **TRIO** set off down to meet Grandpa Angus. When they arrived at Westie Woods, Grandpa Angus was nowhere to be seen.

There was a **NOTE attached** to Daisy's windscreen wipers which read:

Dear Roobie and Radley,
Please choose a Christmas tree and put it up on the roof.
THANKS.
I will come and collect it later.
Love Grandpa xx

6 Noises In The Woods

Roobie climbed carefully up onto the **ROOF** of the campervan. She had found a long piece of thick, blue rope she had often seen Grandpa Angus use for securing things. **(He was always finding and collecting items in the camper for one of his recycling projects.)** She threw one end of the rope down towards Radley and Disco.

'Tie this around the tree, and I will pull it up, and you push from your end,' she shouted.

'No problem,' said Radley with a gulp.

He gave one end of the rope to Disco, who placed it into his mouth, and then to his surprise, suddenly did an **ALMIGHTY** leap up into the air, spun around several times, and lassoed the middle and both ends of the Christmas tree, just like he had seen cowboys do in films.

'WOW, that was totally awesome!' said Radley, chuckling.

Roobie pulled with all her might, and Radley and Disco pushed the tree upwards.

'Heave-Ho,'

'Heave-Ho,'

'Heave-Ho up you go!' they shouted together.

The tree was now up on top of the roof and Roobie **SECURED** it in place with the rope so that it wouldn't move.

'That's it then. Off we go home.'

'What about the **Christmas presents?**' asked Radley.

'Santa will bring those tonight, when we are all tucked up, sleeping in our beds,' replied Roobie.

'Oooh, no – the presents over there!' he exclaimed and pointed towards the direction of just behind the campervan.

Roobie and Disco both looked and saw brightly-wrapped Christmas presents laying in the snow **SCATTERED** all around the trees.

The little **TRIO** walked excitedly towards them. Disco squealed with delight, throwing his little trotters up into the air, spinning around several times on the spot, and then **SOMERSAULTING** forward to the next spot.

'They look like they've been sprinkled with icing sugar, like the mince pies that we sell at the bakery. There isn't too much snow on them, so they **CAN'T** have been here that long,' said Roobie.

They began to investigate further and found a trail of more presents. Some of them were lying in the snow, the rest balanced on **LOW** branches.

Roobie suddenly spotted a present lying just on top of a nearby **holly bush,** the wrapping paper partly ripped open, exposing one bright pink furry slipper.

'Ooh, this is exactly like the style **Grandma Soozie** wears. I wonder where the other one is?' she exclaimed.

'OVER HERE,' grunted Disco, picking up in his mouth a pink soggy matching slipper from right under the bottom of the bush.

'Good job I'm small. I can see underneath things much **BETTER** than you can,' he snorted.

Roobie looked up and studied the higher snowy branches of some of the trees. She could see that there were several which had presents hanging down.

'SUGAR ME TIMBERS!' shouted Radley loudly. **(He had been reading a lot of pirate adventure books recently, and this was one of many of his latest sayings.)**

'Where do you think all these have come from, Roobie Roo?'

'I don't know: it seems very strange,' she replied.

'Shall we **START** opening them?' asked Radley.

Roobie examined one of the presents, and saw that there was a gift tag attached, which read, **'Happy Christmas Thomas, love Mum and Dad.'**

'No! These are not our presents to open. They belong to someone else, so it would be WRONG to open them.'

Radley looked thoughtful.

'Let's pick them all up then and take them back to Daisy.'

'I suppose at least they will be **SAFE** then,' said Roobie.

When he heard that Roobie thought this was a good idea of his, Radley shut his eyes and gave out a **BEAMING** pleased-with-himself smile.

'Oh, what fun. I just love presents!' squealed Disco, spinning around several times on the spot.

They began to pick up the presents, their little feet **CRUNCHING** as they moved backwards and forwards in the snow. They soon realised that there were quite a few more to **COLLECT** than they had first thought.

'This is going take **AGES**,' said Radley.

'I have a good idea,' said Roobie. 'We will go and fetch our wagon we use for deliveries. It's in **DAISY.** We can **LOAD** them up quicker then.'

'Grrrrrrrrrrrreat idea,' said Radley. 'The quicker we pick them up the better – my paws are **frrrreezing**,' his teeth chattering as he spoke.

They **QUICKLY** managed to pick up most of the parcels they could reach and loaded them into their cart, and then **PACKED** them safely onto the seats in the campervan.

Just as they were loading up the last cart, they heard a loud, unfamiliar noise. It made them all **STOP** and **STAND STILL** in their tracks. They all moved their eyes backwards and forwards and looked at each other with startled expressions.

'What was that?' cried Radley.

'No idea,' said Roobie.

'It came from over there!' **SQUEALED** Disco, pointing towards the direction where they had just collected the Christmas presents from.

They heard it again. It sounded like something or someone was shrieking out. Radley and Roobie **FROZE** to the spot. Disco, suddenly and without warning, jumped up onto Radley's shoulders with such a leap that his two front wellington boots flew off his trotters!

Roobie put her paw up to her mouth, in a motion to **signal** to Radley and Disco to keep very quiet. They **NODDED** to her to indicate they understood.

They began to walk forward, in a slow, **CREEPING motion** to keep the sound of their movements to a minimum.

Disco was making little gentle **SNUFFLING** noises with his breathing.

Radley felt as if his **HEART** was in his mouth. Roobie appeared to be the bravest of the trio, but inwardly she could feel the **BEATING** of her heart in her ribcage.

The nearer to the trees they got, the **LOUDER** the sounds **GREW**.

Radley thought to himself that the noise sounded a bit like the bellowing that he had heard Farmer McGruff's **Highland cattle** make. He really hoped that it wasn't his cattle, as he was secretly quite scared of them. They had two big horns on top of their head and reminded him of the time he had been chased back in the summer when he and his friend **Archy Turner** had helped themselves to some of Farmer McGruff's **APPLES.**

Oh, dear he thought. Perhaps the cattle had **ESCAPED** from the farm, or worse still, had got through the fence and into the woods where they were. Radley felt worried.

JUST what were those **NOISES?**

7 Moonlight Rainbows

They were now in a **DENSE** part of the woods. The vast number of trees in this area made it very dark, and difficult to see.

Roobie suddenly remembered that she still had her little **TORCH**, which Santa had given her as a present when they had visited him. She gently reached down with her paw into her **JACKET** pocket, feeling for it, and gently pulled it out.

Radley, seeing what she had done, and without a word being **SPOKEN**, managed to copy her and do the same.

Armed with their torches, they switched them on at the same time and shone them over towards the direction of the trees. The beams formed **TWO** arches of **BRILLIANT** white light. Then, as if by **MAGIC**, they changed into the most magnificent colours. The clump of Christmas trees that stood before them looked as if it was decorated with hundreds of coloured fairy lights.

'WOAH, it's a rainbow!' squealed out Disco in delight.

'Sssh, be quiet,' whispered Roobie.

Radley whispered back, 'There are eyes, Roobs. **Pairs of eyes** looking at us. **LOTS!'**

Roobie was now standing, partly hidden behind a large oak tree. Radley and Disco crouched down, so they stayed hidden behind a **CLUMP** of branches near the ground. Radley could feel Disco **QUIVERING**, and not knowing if this was from **FEAR**, or the cold, he reached down with his small paw and gently touched the top of Disco's head to comfort him.

Disco was startled by this, not knowing in the darkness what it was that had touched him. Just as he was about to let out an almighty squeal of **FRIGHT**, they heard several loud voices crying out, to their surprise, their own names, followed by:

'IT'S US!'

'REMEMBER US?'

Roobie and Radley, now they could see a bit better, **PEERED** towards the trees. In front of them they could see several pairs of deep, twinkling black eyes peering back at them. There were also faces, dark brown furry ones!

'Reindeer, Roobs. It's reindeer. Only **BIG BROWN, FLUFFYTASTIC, FLIPPING REINDEER!'** whispered Radley.

Stepping out towards them from the middle of the trees came a reindeer with **bits of Christmas tree sticking out of his ears!**

'Pleased to meet you, Master Radley,' said the reindeer, shaking his paw.

'Roobie Roo, hello, and of course Disco. We have met before, when you came to see Santa. **I'm PRANCER,'** he said.

'I'm DANCER,' said a reindeer who was lying right on the very top of the dense Christmas trees. He looked as if he was swinging in a garden hammock.

'VIXEN,' came a voice from an upside-down reindeer. 'I have branches that are tickling my **nether regions!'** and then he let out several giggles.

'DASHER here!' A deep muffled voice spoke from the back of the trees.

'I really need to get myself out of here quickly!' By the strange expression on his face, it looked like

this needed to take place **SOONER** rather than later!

'**PHEW,** thank goodness it's just you guys that we've found,' said Roobie, letting a long sigh of relief out.

'**AYE**, you did scare us. You really did!' Radley informed Prancer.

'Yep, I was so scared that I lost two of my wellington boots – they shot right off my trotters!' Disco snorted.

Prancer gave Disco a puzzled look.

'**HEY**, look. We need to get out of these trees **RIGHT NOW!**' shouted Dasher in a booming voice, making sure that everyone could hear him!

'Keep your antlers on, old boy!' shouted Prancer.

'Right, come on, Roobie and Radley, let's start pulling these fellas out.'

They began to **RESCUE** the reindeer from the trees one at a time. As each one of them became free, there became more help available to reach the more difficult ones. There were lots of branches to move out of the way and buckets of snow **(although they didn't actually have any buckets!).**

Some needed pulling and others needed pushing to get them out. Several of the reindeer were more difficult to reach than others, such as Dancer who was laying right at the very top of the trees. **(Secretly, he wasn't really stuck, but enjoyed making a lot of noise and fuss, so the others thought he was!)**

'Right, is that everyone?' asked Roobie.

'Let's do a head count,' said Blitzen.

'Or should we say an **antler count?**' chuckled Cupid.

'Line up everyone!' shouted Blitzen.

'We do this at school. We **SHOUT** our names out, so the teacher knows that we are there,' said Radley.

'All of this sounds a bit like my time when I was in the **MILITARY**.

I was an especially important reindeer, I'll have you know. They used me on **TOP SECRET** snow operations!' said Prancer.

'I think that with my experience, I should be in **CHARGE** now!' he said, puffing out his chest. **(Nobody responded to Prancer's request that he should be in charge.)**

'Don't get him started on telling those old military war stories,' said Vixen.

'Otherwise we will be here **all night!**' said Dasher.

All the other reindeer **(apart from Prancer)** laughed out loud to this.

Finally, standing in a single file line up in front of them, were the following:

'Where is **Rudolph**?' exclaimed Comet.

All the reindeer looked around, staring **BLANKLY** at each other.

'Well, Rudolph **SET** off with us, didn't he?' Donner replied.

'Yes, he was right up at the front with his shiny **RED NOSE**,' said Vixen.

Blitzen sighed loudly and said in his deep voice, 'Rudolph is only really needed to guide the sleigh when it is **FOGGY**, but Santa can never tell when that might be. So, he is always up at the front just in case!'

'So, it's just like in the Christmas song,' said Roobie, and the three of them began to sing.

Rudolph, the red nose reindeer.
Had a very shiny nose.
And if you ever saw him,
You would even say it glows.
All of the other reindeer—

'Hey, **STOP**. There is no time for any singing!' shouted Prancer.

'Where is Rudolph now then?' asked Roobie.

Prancer nervously started scratching his antlers. 'I really don't know where he is, but more importantly, where is **SANTA**?'

8 The Search for Rudolph And Santa

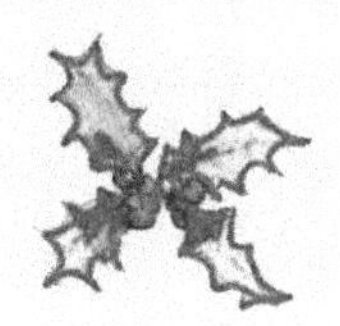

'So, tell us what happened, Prancer. Why were you **HIDING** in the trees, here in Westie Woods?' asked Radley.

Dasher said, 'I'll tell you, little fellow. And a **lot faster** than Prancer, with his **BLOOMING** long-winded story telling!'

Prancer gave Dasher one of his best **ICY** reindeer stares, one which let him know that there was no way he was going to let anyone else tell the story. Prancer could be very bossy towards the other reindeer sometimes. But deep down, he had a **KIND** heart, and loved all the other reindeer, although he would never have admitted this.

Prancer took in a **DEEP BREATH** and said, 'We were flying in the sleigh, high up in the sky, Santa, Rudolph, all of us together. We had been delivering Christmas presents to the other side of the world, and we were on our way back According to our **COMPASS,** we had just entered back into the United Kingdom.'

Dasher interrupted, 'There was a **BIG** shooting star!'

Comet said, 'It was **ENORMOUS!**'

Prancer shot out **TWO** more of his icy reindeer stares at Dasher and Comet, and then continued. 'Santa was **BLINDED by the light** from the star, and then he couldn't see where he was going.'

'Then all we saw were lots of **STARS,**' said Comet.

'**OH**, and it was **soooooo** dark,' Donner added.

Prancer's top lip raised slightly at one corner, showing just a glimpse of his teeth **(this was a sign he was beginning to get annoyed!).**

There were ripples of other comments, which went whirling around, and then they bounced back again like a boomerang, coming from other reindeer that were standing listening.

'Boy, it was dark!'

'So dark!'

'Dark and scary!'

'Scary and dark!'

'So dark!'

'Dark!'

Vixen suddenly **PUFFED** out his chest and stood up straight, which made him feel a bit taller! He was a reindeer of few words, but when he felt he had something to say, he would **SAY** it.

He cleared his throat and said, **'Listen in everybody!'**

Not a single antler twitched, or whisker moved as he said this.

SNOW was still gently falling all around, and a few flakes landed on the end of Vixen's nose which he licked to moisten his mouth. All eyes were fixed on him.

'Might I suggest that we all spread out in **PAIRS** and start searching for Rudolph and

Santa. So we don't get lost, might I also suggest that we use our **jingle bells** around our necks, so we can hear where we are.' **(Vixen had a tone to his voice, and the other reindeer often called him posh!)**

Roobie whispered to Radley, 'Well, we don't have any jingle bells!'

Disco suddenly squealed with excitement.

'Yes, we do, I have my **jingle bell** around my neck which Santa gave me!' With this he did a little Scottish jig on the spot, and the little bell tinkled and rang out a jingle.

'Perfect, simply **PERFECT**,' said Roobie.

The **SEARCH PARTY** set off, all the Reindeer in pairs, and Roobie, Radley and Disco as a trio. They spread out and began to search. They could hear the repeated echo of **Rudolph's and Santa's** names, as they heard the Reindeer shouting them out around the woods.

'Let's look for **FOOTPRINTS**,' said Radley.

'Yes, Santa will surely have left **BIG** boot prints in the snow,' said Roobie.

'I'll keep my snout to the ground,' grunted Disco as he began sniffing with his **SNOUT** close to the snow, ploughing up drifts of snow as if he had a digger on the end of his snout, and then shaking them back off. He was now back wearing all **FOUR** of his wellingtons again, but the snow was so deep in places you couldn't see them.

'Now, no wandering off you two. **Let's keep together**. We don't want to add you to the search for Santa and Rudolph,' Roobie said, looking at Radley and Disco.

There was now a **THICK** blanket of snow, and further snowflakes kept falling. The silvery moon above their heads seemed as if it was following them, as they made their way in the soft snow.

Roobie and Radley continued searching, their eyes assisted by their coloured torches. Who would have thought how **USEFUL** these had turned out to be?

Close to where they had earlier found and picked up Christmas presents, Disco started making a loud **OINK, OINK** noise. He had found something with his snout. Digging in the one spot, he suddenly threw up into the air a large, brightly coloured **UMBRELLA!**

'This is like the one that Grandpa Angus uses for **FISHING**,' snorted Disco. He

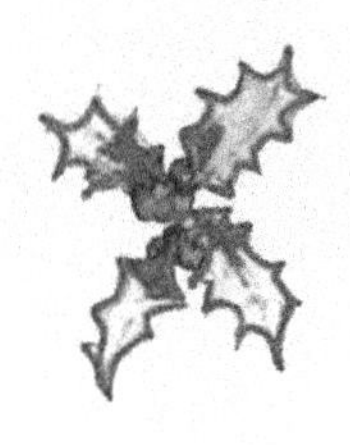

began to use the umbrella as a walking stick. His legs were only little, and his belly was near to the ground, which made walking difficult in the snow, so for him, finding the umbrella was a **LUCKY** find.

'We must have been this way before, then,' said Roobie.

'**AYE**, indeed we have. It appears that we have gone around in a complete circle! I can see **Daisy,**' Radley said as he peered into the distance through a gap in the nearby hedge.

'UH-OH!' he exclaimed.

'What is it?' Roobie asked in a quiet voice.

'There are lights on in the campervan, and I can hear voices,' he replied.

Radley suddenly whispered to Disco, '**Pssst...**pass me the umbrella.'

Disco now felt frozen to the spot with fear. He was holding the umbrella carefully in his mouth. He managed to move his head skilfully and slowly towards Radley, who managed to just reach out and **GRAB** it.

Roobie, with her eyes fixed, watched Radley's black shadow against the white snow as he moved. He looked enormous, like a **BIG** monster, as he took big steps in the deep snow. Every time he took another step, he had to **SHAKE** the heavy snow off each of his wellingtons before he could take another.

Armed with the umbrella, Radley reached the **GAP** in the hedge. He stood with his back against the hedge and positioned his head, so that he could see, but not be seen **(he had watched action films on TV where he had seen them do this).**

Radley felt scared. He could feel the sound of his beating heart against his rib cage: **LUB-dub-LUB-dub-LUB-dub.**

He screwed his eyes up and peered through the falling snowflakes towards Daisy the campervan.

'WHOA!' he said, in a much louder voice than he had intended to.

Roobie and Disco moved forward. They were both now standing next to Radley, and they were all looking at the same thing.

From the light shining out from inside the campervan, they could see, sitting on a bright turquoise camping stool, a **BIG BROWN FLUFFYTASTIC FLIPPING REINDEER.**

They **CLIMBED** through the gap in the hedge and made their way towards Daisy. As they drew nearer, they could see that the reindeer had a bright **RED nose** which was **GLOWING**.

When they came face to face with the reindeer, it continued sitting on the camping stool. They could see that it was sipping tea from a mug which they recognised belonged in the campervan.

'RUDOLPH?' said Roobie in a loud voice.

With this, the reindeer sprang up from the stool, and in doing so, spilled quite a bit of tea all over himself.

'Oh, I'm so very pleased to meet you,' he said, **MOPPING** up the tea he had spilled with what looked like Grandpa Angus's Scarf, which he was wearing.

Radley narrowed his eyes and focused on the tea-stained scarf.

'I'm such a **CLUMSY OLD SAUSAGE!**' said Rudolph, looking down at the stains.

Radley was about to voice his concern because he knew that this **WAS** Grandpa Angus's favourite **West Highland Wanderers** supporters' scarf.

Radley suddenly came to his senses, and heard the voice inside his head say, 'This is only a Rudolph the red nose **FLUFFYTASTIC, FLIPPING** Reindeer. Oh, **WOW**, I am actually with Rudolph the red nosed reindeer – how **COOL** is this. In fact, this is totally **AWESOME.** What did a few tea stains matter? I am CLUMSY and MESSY. Mother is always telling me this!'

So instead, Radley found himself saying, 'Oh, don't worry, Rudolph. I am sure the tea stains will all come out in the **WASH!**'

Before Rudolph could say anymore, they heard another much deeper voice say, '**RUDOLPH** and I have had quite a **SHOCK!**'

Roobie and Radley looked at each other, and then they heard Disco squealing in an excited manner. In fact, he was so excited he couldn't speak.

They peered into the campervan. The sliding door was open. To their astonishment, sitting on the **Buddy Box** seat was a man wearing big black boots, a red suit edged with white fur and he had a white hair and beard.

The three of them all said at the same time, **'SANTA!!!'**

9 The Tree of Awesomeness

'Where are the **OTHER** Reindeer?' asked Rudolph.

'They're out searching for **YOU!**' Roobie informed him.

Rudolph suddenly reached up and pressed the end of his ruby red glowing nose.

'**WOW**, that's an **AWESOME** nose you've got there, Rudolph! I wish mine glowed like that,' said Radley.

'It acts like a homing device. I'm the **MOST** important reindeer of course, as I guide the sleigh. When I press my nose, the other reindeer know which direction to follow and it makes me easy to see!'

'So, they'll know how to find you now, will they?' asked Roobie.

Rudolph **RAISED** his eyebrows slightly and looked at Roobie. He didn't speak, as he didn't need to. Within a matter of minutes, the other **EIGHT** reindeer from the search party had returned and were standing around them.

Looking at the mug of tea that Rudolph was holding, Dasher said, '**Oooh**, is there any **TEA?**'

'**NO...**only two cups,' said Santa.

'That's a shame,' said Cupid, pouting his lips together to make the shape of a **LOVE HEART** between his top and bottom lips.

'All that searching for you two was thirsty work!'

He made several deliberate **DRY** mouth sounds with his mouth. He looked at **BOTH** Rudolph and Santa again and looked longingly at their tea. He had secretly hoped they might give him a sip.

'There is **NO TIME** to be standing around drinking tea!' **SHOUTED** Prancer in his bossy voice.

Santa looked up from his now-empty mug, with what looked like **TEARS** in his eyes. He took a deep intake of breath and began to **TWIZZLE** both ends of his big white whiskers on his moustache.

A few moments later he eventually, in a crestfallen voice, said several times, **'What to do,** what to do...**what am I going to do?'**

He looked thoughtful as if he was in a world of his own, his eyes glazed over, and he gave a **BIG** sigh.

'What's wrong, Santa?' asked Roobie, sensing Santa's upset.

'The sleigh – it's **DEFUNKLED,** Roobs, it's not going anywhere!' he replied.

'Defunkled! What does that mean?' asked Radley.

'It's broken, damaged beyond immediate repair, young Master Radley,' replied Santa.

There was quite a pause while Radley thought about what he had just heard Santa say to him. Then he **LOOKED** into Santa's eyes with a **SAD** look on his face.

'Does that mean you **WON'T** be delivering any more Christmas presents then?' asked Radley.

'Yes, that's a **BIG NO-NO.** In fact, AN IMPOSSIBILITY!' replied Santa.

The cold air filled with loud gasps from the Reindeer as they listened to what Santa had said.

'WOAH!'

'NO WAY!'

'Nooooooo!'

'GEEZ!'

Radley drew in a deep breath and **SIGHED** heavily, as he let it back out again into the cold night air. His breath was clearly visible in a small white cloud around his mouth.

Rudolph, suddenly without warning, sprang up from the camping stool. He cleared his throat and shouted in a loud booming voice, **'IN THE HISTORY OF CHRISTMAS,** this **CANNOT** and will **NOT HAPPEN!'**

There were more **LOUD** gasps from the rest of the Reindeer!

'We need to come up with a plan, and quickly. We all need to put our **THINKING CAPS** on!' said Rudolph.

Radley, feeling **CONFUSED,** looked over at Roobie. 'Have we got any of those caps?' he asked.

'It's a **figure of speech.** Adults tend to say things that express things, but they don't actually require them to be done,' she replied.

'So, we don't actually have to put caps on our heads then?' asked Radley.

'No,' replied Roobie, chuckling to herself.

Disco **(who was super intelligent, as most pigs are)** let out several snorts of laughter. '**HEH, HEH,** no we don't,' he snorted. '**HEE, HEE, HEE!**'

Radley frowned and looked at Disco, unsure if he was laughing at him, or at the silly saying about the thinking caps that Rudolph had mentioned. Disco was his pet as well as his **best friend**, so he dismissed the fact he was laughing at him. He will be laughing at that silly old sausage Rudolph, he thought to himself.

'AWESOME,' said Radley in a **LOUD** Scottish voice which echoed!

Just had he had said the word **AWESOME,** he felt the snowy ground under his feet begin to shake. His feet and legs felt like they were wobbling like a jelly.

At first, they heard a humming that grew louder, and then the humming changing into a **SING SONG** voice, which said, 'I am the Westie of Wisdom. You have spoken the word **'awesome'** one thousand times and you have now unlocked **THE MAGICAL POWERS OF THE TREE OF AWESOMENESS**. You are **free to dream of SHOOTING STARS,** and **ADVENTURES!** Whenever you need help, you may use these magical powers.'

Radley looked over at Roobie and Disco, whose mouths were wide open with astonishment. Then he looked at the reindeer and Santa.

'Well that's just **AWESOME,** isn't it?' said Radley, laughing.

Just then, the starry midnight blue sky above them suddenly started to change colour to a much brighter blue. All the trees around them started to sway and the branches began to **SHAKE** the snow from them.

Roobie looked over at Radley, who was busy brushing snow from his jacket.

'Quick, let's get into Daisy,' said Roobie.

The little trio **RAN** as fast as they could in the snow and jumped into the front seats. Roobie sat in the driver's seat and Radley in the passenger seat with Disco sitting on his lap.

'Fasten your seat belts – I think we are about to have **LIFT OFF!**' shouted Roobie.

With this, **BIG** clouds of rainbow-coloured smoke started to gush out from both the engine bay and the **exhaust pipe**, completely covering the reindeer and sleigh. Santa sat in the sleigh in the **ready for lift off** position, firmly holding the reins, his eyes fixed on Daisy's rear engine door. They **WAITED** and **waited** and **WAITED,** but nothing!

Roobie looked over at Radley.

'Say it again!' she shouted.

But before Radley could say a word, the sleigh began to move slowly forward with a **BUMPETY BUMP, BUMPETY BUMP** as it hit some hard lumps of frozen snow. This was followed by the sound of **BANG…WHIZZ…BANG…WHIZZ,** which sounded like a firework rocket exploding. They looked in the mirrors to see lots of sparks of different colours flying out behind them.

Daisy's engine was making loud purring noises that only an air-cooled engine can make with its air puffs. **'Putt-Putt-Putt, Putt-Putt-Putt.'**

Then there was a tremendous **WHOOOOOOSH** followed by a loud **SWOOSH, WHOOSH, SWOOSH, WHOOSH.**

'Whassat?' said Radley, sitting bolt upright in his seat.

They felt movement as Daisy campervan begin to raise her front nose into the air and then all **FOUR WHEELS** were up off the snowy ground. Daisy's wheels began to spin around and around, although they were not actually needed now, because they were up in the air **FLYING.** Behind them they were pulling Santa in his Sleigh and nine **BIG, BROWN, FURRYTASTIC, FLIPPING REINDEER!**

'WOW, WOW, WOW. Look, we are really flying,' said Roobie.

They were flying high up above **Westie Woods.** Radley, feeling brave as he could be, looked out of the window to the view below of snowy roofs and tops of trees.

It's a magical night, magical night.
Daisy campervan takes to her flight.
Santa, the reindeer behind in a row.
Rooftops below them, covered in snow.
The adventure begins, gifts piled up high.
Whooshing and swooshing, in the night sky.
Lots of snowflakes and stars shooting past.
They travel on their journey ever so fast.
With AWESOME magical powers from the tree.
Roobie, Radley, Disco...keeping safe all three.

Roobie nervously glanced in the rear-view mirror and saw Rudolph's red nose glowing brightly behind them.

They were flying through big

SWIRLING

snowy white fluffytastic clouds which had flashes of bright colours

WHIZZING

along the side of them which came from

magical powers.

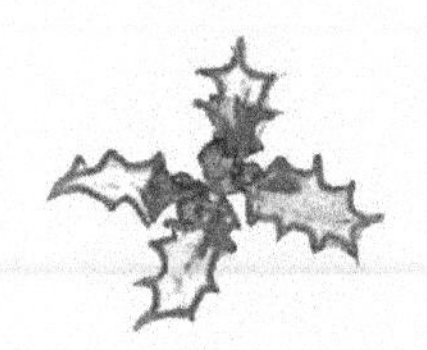

They then heard a **GIGANTIC THUD** on the roof, then more **THUD, THUD, THUDS.**

'What is that?' squealed Disco, his trotters locking up tightly on Radley's lap.

'I don't know, but it sounded like we might have hit something!' cried Radley.

'Well, whatever it is, it must be something **ENORMOUS** from the sound it made,' cried Roobie.

BONE5

10 Up, Up And Away

'I'M SCARED,' cried Roobie, as she grabbed onto the steering wheel a bit tighter with her paws.

'Don't be scared, Roobs, this is **AWESOME!**' shouted Radley.

'It's saying **that word** in the first place that's got us into this situation!' she shouted back at him.

'I think you mean it's thanks to me that we are HELPING Santa deliver Christmas presents to all the children, who, without our help, would not be getting any!' Radley said in an even louder voice.

'We are doing the **CHRISTMAS CAMPERVAN RESCUE,**' squealed Disco, making excited oinking noises.

'**Sssh,** listen,' said Radley.

There was a **LOUD** sound of knocking. **TAP, TAP, TAP,** followed by a **RAP, RAP, RAP.** Radley looked over into the back of the camper where the Christmas Presents were piled up high.

Then he heard it again. **TAP, TAP, TAP,** followed by a **RAP, RAP, RAP.** Radley undid his seat belt and made his way into the back of the camper, closely followed by Disco.

Disco, who was right behind Radley, gently **TUGGED** on his tail. Radley turned around immediately, and saw that it was Disco, with his head looking up towards the middle of the roof, where there was a large glass **SUNROOF.**

Radley stared up and peered with his eyes into the darkness.

'**WELL, SHIVER ME TIMBERS!'** Staring down at him with its face pressed flat against the glass with a round squashed nose, and a pair of dark twinkling eyes, was only a **BIG, BROWN, FLUFFYTASTIC, FLIPPING REINDEER!** Radley recognised him – it was **Prancer!** Radley wondered how he had got onto the roof.

Prancer, delighted that he had gained Radley's attention, opened up his eyes wider and moved them towards where the catch was to indicate to open up the sunroof.

'He wants to **COME IN!**' squealed Disco excitedly, and suddenly jumped over onto the campervan worktops. From there, he did a **GIGANTIC** leap, landing by grabbing Radley's ears to pull himself up onto his shoulders.

'OUCH! Mind my **LUG HOLES!'** screeched Radley, feeling the pain of having his ears pulled.

The two of them wobbled backwards and forwards like they were practising some sort of balancing act you would see in a **CIRCUS**. This was made much more difficult of course by the speed they were **FLYING** at!

Disco tried with all his might to stretch up and reach the catch, but it was no good. The wobbling continued like the most **WOBBLISH JELLY** on a plate, and then, a cry of **WHOA** and **YIKES!** as Disco toppled off and fell backwards. **KLUNK!** He landed, **PLOP,** straight into the basin of the little stainless-steel sink. He quickly managed to grab onto the tap to pull himself back up.

Radley managed to move a few Christmas presents and push them together to make himself a **PLATFORM,** so he was higher. He climbed up and positioned himself with his back towards the sink.

'Come on, **jump on**, and don't pull my ears this time!'

This time Disco climbed on **(without pulling Radley's ears)** and they managed to move carefully towards the sunroof. Disco hit the catch first time with his trotters and the roof sprang open. Prancer dived head first down through the sunroof into the camper, **SNAPPING it** shut behind him.

'Right, my furry little chums, I have come to get operation **Christmas Campervan Rescue** on track. I suggested to Santa that you would need some help. And of course, I'm the best reindeer for job,' said Prancer in his bossy voice. With this he moved forward into the cab area and **SLAPPED** a small round device onto the dashboard. It had red lights flashing up and down on it and was making a strange **BLOOP, BLEEP** noise.

'This is a **NORAD** Santa tracking device – only one in existence in the world!'

'**WOW,** what does that do then?' asked Roobie, who was feeling a lot more relaxed now that Prancer was on board with them.

'It tracks everything that flies in defence of the **USA** and **Canada**, 24 hours a day, **365** days of the year: and that includes Santa.'

'That's totally **AMAZING**,' gasped Radley (avoiding the use of his other 'A' word).

'The **HEAD ELF** of the sleigh launch party places it into the sleigh when Santa sets off, so then children all around the world can track where Santa is,' Prancer explained.

'So, will **NORAD** know where Santa is again now?' asked Radley.

'Well, Santa seems hopeful that now we are up and moving again that they will. Santa has no set pattern of delivery. He has his favourite places he likes to go, but always makes the **DECISION** after he sets off, and this is also depending on the weather.'

'What about the crash Santa had, will **NORAD** know about that?' asked Radley.

'You certainly like to ask a lot of **QUESTIONS,** young Master Radley. They will probably think that Santa was having a long tea break,' replied Prancer.

'Right, we have a lot to get through, and a lot of tricky locations to travel to tonight. Thankfully it's just the **United Kingdom** we have to deliver to now. Roobie Roo, when Rudolph flashes his nose twice, he means it's time to stop for a delivery. Have you got that?'

'AYE, AYE CAPTAIN PRANCER. Two flashes means time to stop!' she said in her soft sing-song, Scottish voice.

They began with deliveries around Westie Green, with Daisy campervan hovering over the snowy rooftops and chimneys of the Westie Hutters' homes. Santa dropped down from his sleigh each time, with some of the **rescue reindeer party** helping by forming a chain to pass down the Christmas presents.

Radley had always wondered to himself how Santa got into houses with no chimneys or houses where the fire was lit. He now knew how: Santa showed him. He had a **MAGIC KEY** that could get him into any locked doors.

Radley thought to himself as he stood on snowy rooftops helping Santa to place presents into the chimneys of his friends, what would Archy and Popsie Turner, Maisy Daisy, the Winfield Westies and Miss Tilly Bean **SAY** if they **KNEW** that he was helping Santa? It was funny to think of them unaware of any of this, all of them tucked up fast asleep in their beds.

They darted and dashed, flying through the night sky as they travelled at speed. From Westie Green they travelled to the **HIGHLANDS,** swooshing left up to **Skye** and the **Outer Hebrides**, then whooshing right around the tops of the **islands of Orkney, Fair Isle and Arran.** Roobie thought to herself that she had seen Grandma Soozie knit sweaters in the styles of Fair Isle and Arran.

They saw **BIG** grey elephants and giraffes down in the **ZOO** as they passed down from **Dundee** and into **Edinburgh** and the castle.

Daisy campervan glistened in the moonlight and the stars twinkled above them in the icy night sky. Roobie was doing a **truly marvellous job**. Radley felt really proud of his sister, who, with the assistance and guidance of Prancer, was hovering above the rooftops keeping the campervan steady as they **DELIVERED** more and more Christmas presents.

They flew over the tops of mountains and peaks in **WALES** and saw lots of sheep sitting in the fields that

looked tiny cotton wool balls from high up in **Daisy** campervan.

There were valleys, rivers and seas to cross over and a stop in the **EMERALD island of IRELAND.** Prancer told them that legend said that there were **Leprechauns,** which were a branch of relatives of the Elves. Radley did his best to see if he could spot some, but you may have guessed, he never did!

There were tall buildings to watch out for, such as **Blackpool Tower.** The flight over **London** was particularly tricky, with Tower Bridge and the London Eye and Big Ben. Roobie and Radley were **AMAZED** at what they were seeing on their flight. They had only ever lived in Westie Green.

The weather conditions kept changing. It was mostly snow that they were flying through, but the wind factor near the sea made flying more difficult.

They were lucky near **Land's End** that a Cornish lighthouse helped them stay on track with its **FLASHING LIGHT.** It guided them, together with Rudolph, safely into land where they needed to move in and do a tricky drop to the **SCILLY ISLES.** Radley and Disco both laughed until tears ran down their faces finding out that there was a place called Silly!

'IT'S A RIGHT PEA SOUPER!' shouted Prancer at the top of his voice.

'Pea Souper – what does that mean?' asked Roobie.

'THICK FOG, down there, just like **PEA SOUP.** Can't see a thing,' said Prancer as he put a rucksack-type bag on his back.

'Time for a **REINDEER STACK.** Goodbye, my furry chums.' With that, he suddenly jumped out of the campervan sliding door!

'Where has he gone?' shouted Radley.

'He's doing a **REINDEER STACK,'** squealed Disco, jumping up and down.

The windscreen wipers had lumps of ice on them the size of ice lollies. They were making a funny noise. **SCHWUMP, SCHWUMP, SCHWUMP. SCHWUMP, SCHWUMP, SCHWUMP,** as they stuck to the bay front screen.

'It must be freezing fog,' Roobie shouted over the noise of the engine. 'I can't see a thing!'

Radley put his **BIG** black nose up to the window and huffed his warm breath in several places. It was just about enough to see Prancer, who was wearing a bright red and green **parachute** which was fully open. He was attached to a thick, stretchy, candy cane-red striped bungee. This was tied to the sleigh being held in place by **DANCER, DASHER AND BLITZEN** who were responsible for the **BOUNCE** action!

COMET, DONNER and **RUDOLPH** remained still to keep the sleigh balanced to prevent it tipping over.

Attached to Prancer's feet, one on each side, were **CUPID** and **VIXEN** who, between them, held Santa's present sack. Holding on to their feet hung Santa!

'**WOW**, so that's a reindeer stack,' they all said together. They also now knew how Santa got to those **tricky** places.

They continued their journey and flew back up the English Channel over Bristol, up to Gloucestershire, Birmingham, Coventry, Derby, Manchester, Liverpool – far too many locations to list them all – until their work was finished.

Rudolph **FLASHED** his shiny red nose in one continuous flicker, which meant one thing. This was the **END** of their deliveries.

11 The Carrot And Mince Pie Party

Rudolph flashed his red nose **TWICE** to indicate that they were over the **NORTH POLE.** This was the drop-off point for Santa and the reindeer. The journey to take Santa back to **LAPLAND** was filled with a mixture of happiness and sadness.

Santa's house was in a **secret location,** which had never been revealed to anyone other than the elves that help him, and of course the reindeer. However, it was necessary for Roobie and Radley to see where this was in order to **DROP** Santa and the reindeer off.

As they dropped down to land, they saw that the sky around them was the most unbelievable assortment of magical colours: purple, green, pink, blues and yellows. The colours **TWISTED** and **SWIRLED** around together like watching a kite dancing in the sky.

'WOWZERS!' said Radley, as Disco, still sitting on his lap, put his trotters up onto the side window for a better look.

'Disco lights!' squealed Disco, clapping his trotters together and making his jingle bell around his neck tinkle.

'It's the **NORTHERN LIGHTS**,' said Roobie.

'Ooooo...how do you know that?' asked Radley.

'I saw them in a book that Grandpa Angus showed me,' replied Roobie.

Radley remained **QUIET** but wondered to himself why he had not seen this book. For now, what he was **watching** was happening right in front of him, which was, in his own words, truly a remarkable display of **AWESOMENESS!**

Daisy campervan dropped down onto the soft snow and they could see **SANTA'S** house; a delightful **wooden log cabin** with thick snow on the roof and there was smoke coming from the chimney. In the windows were red and green tartan curtains. Santa's house would not have looked out of place among the wooden huts in Westie Green, thought Roobie.

Just behind the house there was a much larger log cabin that had a sign which read, **'SANTA'S WORKSHOP.'**

'This is just how I imagined Santa's house would be,' said Roobie to Radley and Disco with a big **BEAMING** grin on her face.

The trio got out of Daisy campervan and saw that Santa had already untied the reindeer. Some of the reindeer were doing **STRETCHING** exercises after their flight.

Santa and Rudolph walked towards them with Prancer doing military marches **TEN** paces behind them, closely followed by the rest of the reindeer.

'Thank you, thank you, thank you, **sooooo** much. You three and Daisy campervan have helped me to **RESCUE** Christmas!' said Santa.

With that, he placed into each of Roobie and Radley's paws a **SILVER** reindeer bell, just like the one Disco already had. Then, standing in a line, Santa placed a red ribbon around each of their necks which had a golden **Santa's workshop** coin hanging from it.

'I usually only put these inside **SPECIAL TOYS** that are made here in my workshop,' said Santa.

'SANTA MEDALS!' said Radley.

'Really?' said Roobie.

'Yes, indeed. my little friends, they are **Santa medals** for the **BRAVERY** and **COURAGE** you showed tonight.'

'Now, young Master Radley, you need to concentrate and be very careful when you use the **'A' (awesome)** word because it is now very powerful. **You MUST only use it when you need help, do you understand?'**

'**AYE** Santa, I do!' said Radley, looking very serious and staring right into Santa's **EYES.**

'Right, how about some **FOOD?** I don't know about you, but I am starving,' said Santa.

'PARTY!' the reindeer all said at the same time.

'Ooooo, I love a party I do!' squealed Disco in excitement.

Roobie and Radley both looked at each other blankly and then at Santa.

'He's never been to one before,' said Roobie.

Santa let out a belly laugh. **HO, HO, HO!**

'Well, he will be at the best one ever now!' said Santa.

Roobie and Radley had a good look around underneath the **Rock & Roll** bed storage. Radley was overjoyed at discovering, in his words, a box of **pirate treasure** under there. He found a folding **BBQ** and a bag of charcoal, and much to Cupid's delight, a picnic hamper with plates and **MORE** cups! Santa put the kettle on, so they could all have a cup of tea this time.

Rudolph exchanged his tea-stained scarf for an apron and a chef's hat (**also belonging to Grandpa Angus)** that they found, and he took charge of the **BBQ.** The reindeer had never seen one before and were excited about some **CARROT burgers** that Radley had suggested they make, using the carrots that children had kindly left out for the reindeer. There were also **MINCE PIES** and bottles of milk.

Roobie found **ketchup** and other sauces for the burgers in the little campervan cupboards.

'I am loving these carrot **BURGLARS**,' said Vixen, to which everyone laughed out loud at his mistake.

'You mean **burgers**,' said Rudolph, with tomato ketchup squishing out of his burger as he bit into it and landing all down the front of Grandpa Angus's apron **(more stains to come out in the wash, thought Radley, laughing to himself!).**

'I am loving this ketchup,' said Santa.

'It's **YUMMYTASTIC!**' said Radley.

All the reindeer laughed out loud and shouted together, **'YUMMYTASTIC!'**

Dasher and Dancer fetched a guitar and sat together on top of Daisy's roof and began playing Christmas **SONGS,** which they all joined in with. Disco danced around **jingling** his bell around, much to the amusement of Santa.

The time came to say **GOODBYE** to Santa and the reindeer and go back home.

'I've had the best night of my life, Santa,' said Roobie.

'**ME TOO**,' said Radley and Disco both at the same time.

They sat in Daisy.

'Time to go home!' Roobie said, looking over at Radley.

'Magical powers, Tree of Awesomeness, **AWESOME,** home to Bones Bakery, Westie Green!' said Radley in a loud voice.

With that, they were surrounded by wonderful clouds of rainbow **SMOKE** and up and off into the wonderful starry midnight blue sky above them. Daisy made her familiar **'Putt-Putt-Putt, Putt-Putt-Putt'** air-cooled engine noises as they went higher into the icy night sky. Down below them they saw in the distance Santa and nine **BIG BROWN, FLUFFYTASTIC, FLIPPING REINDEER** waving together back at them.

Within what seemed like a **blink of an eye**, they were flying up above the snowy rooftops of Westie Green and Westie Woods. They could see magnificent views right over the sparkling water of Westie Green Loch glistening in the snow. They could see a thin trail of **SMOKE** coming from Grandpa Angus's house.

'I wonder if Grandpa Angus has been **LOOKING** for Daisy and his Christmas tree?' said Radley.

'Or worse, if he has been looking for us,' said Roobie.

'What time is it now? Have we **MISSED** Christmas?' asked Radley.

She looked at the small clock on the dashboard.

'No, it's 2am. It's Christmas Day!' replied Roobie.

'MERRY CHRISTMAS,' they said out loudly to each other at the same time!

They landed surprisingly softly in the snow right by **THE TREE OF AWESOMENESS**, the Christmas tree still looking as good as it had when they had put it on the roof.

'Where shall we put the tree?' asked Radley.

With this, **DAISY'S** wheels started to turn ever so slowly on the soft snow and reverse them back into the space in the middle of the tree.

'Well, I guess that's our answer. We'll leave her just here,' replied Roobie.

'AMAZING. Grandpa Angus will perhaps think he forgot where he parked it,' said Radley.

'Aye, we can hope. I'm too **TIRED** to worry about it just now. It is well over our bedtime,' said Roobie.

Radley, however, was a little **WORRIED** about Grandpa Angus and what questions he might ask them. Where would they say they had been? Who would believe them. But for now, his **FURRY** eyelids were feeling heavy – he needed to sleep.

The trio crept very quietly back into the Bones Bakery so not to wake anyone, and into the warm cosy lounge where there was a **ROARING** fire. By the light of the fire, they could their stockings hanging up on the **FIREPLACE.** They all **looked** at each other and back at their stockings. They were just as they had hung them up – **EMPTY!** The Christmas tree lights were on and twinkling, but instead of the usual Christmas presents that were piled up after Santa visited, there was nothing!

'**SANTA** has forgotten us!' said Radley.

'Well, we were helping him, weren't we? And we know that Santa **NEVER** visits if you are not asleep, so he couldn't leave us anything,' said Roobie.

'I was **HOPING** that Santa would have brought Grandpa Angus a torch like ours,' said Radley, with a sad look on his face.

'Never mind. There is always **NEXT YEAR**. I am sure he will understand, and we have our silver bells and Santa medals so it's not so bad,' said Roobie.

They carefully climbed the snowy ladder and walked along the large branch which lead into their brightly painted **TREE HUT** bedroom at the back of the bakery.

They were all extremely tired from their **ADVENTURE.** Radley threw all his clothes off in a pile and jumped straight into his crocodile bed and within minutes was fast asleep.

However, Roobie and Disco were distracted by the light of the moon, which was shining **BRIGHT**. They looked out of the window together and in the middle of the moon, it looked like they could see a **BLACK SHADOW** of Santa in his sleigh and the reindeer. They were seeing things – it couldn't possibly be **SANTA.** It had been a long night – time for **BED.**

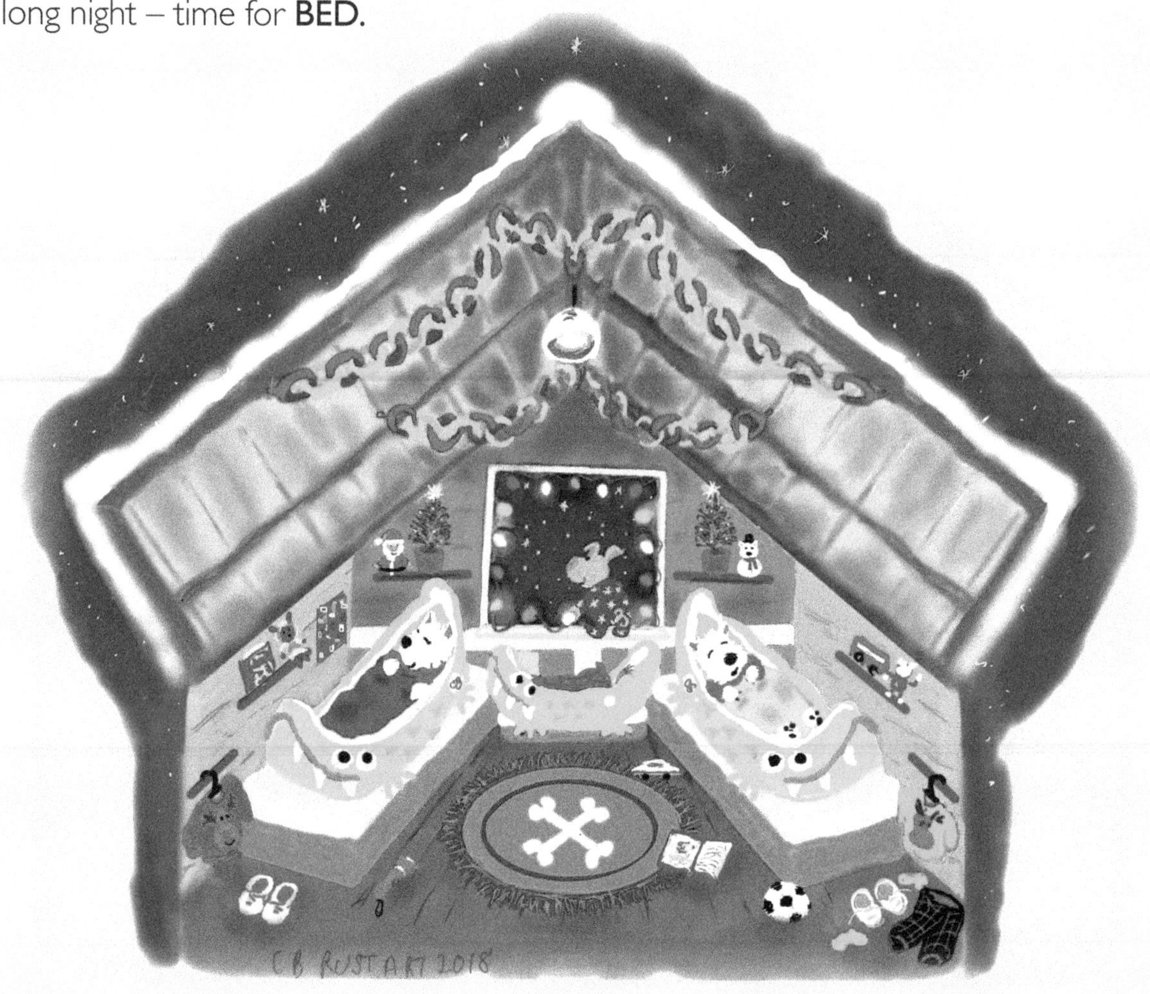

12 Christmas Day in Westie Green

They were woken by the sound of their names being shouted **LOUDLY** up to their bedroom. It was Grandpa Angus's voice. Fearing the worse, they quickly **SCAMPERED** down the winding wooden staircase and opened the door. Standing in their fluffytastic dressing gowns were their mother and father and Grandpa Angus and Grandma Soozie, who were **STAYING** with them for Christmas.

'MERRY CHRISTMAS,' they all shouted together.

'We wondered if you sleepy heads were ever going to wake up this morning,' said Father.

'SANTA has **BEEN,'** said Grandpa Angus, grinning ear to ear.

To their disbelief, on the fireplace were their **HUNG** stockings filled up to the top. Under the Christmas tree there were presents wrapped in brightly coloured Christmas paper with their names on.

Disco did several **CARTWHEELS** around the room squealing, 'He's been, he's been, Santa's been!'

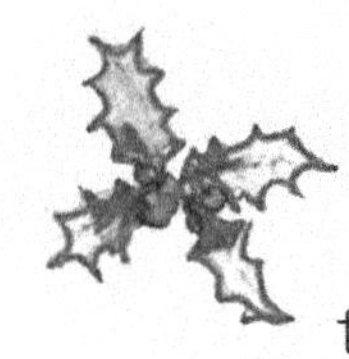

There was much **RIPPING** and **TEARING** of paper for the next hour as they discovered what Santa had brought. Radley got his **FOOTBALL** boots, Roobie the paints that she liked, and they had a knitted teddy each that they had seen in the **WOOLLY BALLS** shop.

Disco had a **NEW SET OF EARS (a pair of headphones)** which played music directly to him. He immediately put them on and started **DANCING.** Everyone laughed as he entered a little world of his own.

Grandpa Angus had a new pocket solar torch, just like the ones they had. Grandma Soozie and their mother had new tartan fluffytastic slippers, scarves and gloves. Everyone was **DELIGHTED** with their gifts from Santa.

After a **BREAKFAST** of Scottish porridge with honey, they had agreed to meet Grandpa Angus outside to help him decorate the Christmas tree. There had been no time to discuss with each other **JUST** how Santa had managed to deliver their Christmas presents after all, or how it was that Daisy was now parked back in her normal place, with the Christmas tree they had left in Westie Woods for Grandpa Angus to collect!!

Outside, they heard Grandpa Angus **WHISTLING** Christmas songs to himself. He had already taken the tree off Daisy's roof and looked pleased to see them arrive to help.

'Aye, it's a lovely tree you picked, my **wee bairns.** A great choice.'

They decorated the tree with lights and lots of other Christmas decorations and it looked **SPLENDID.** The best bit was, Grandpa Angus didn't mention Daisy or the Christmas tree, much to their relief!

Before everyone started arriving for the party, they had one **SPECIAL** Christmas gift to deliver. They walked down the snowy path which led to Westie Green Meadow. Standing by a gap in the snowy stone wall they shouted, **'Merry Christmas, JEANIE'.**

A beautiful dark brown **DONKEY** galloped across the meadow and placed her head over the wall, so they could pat her nose and soft fur. Radley wrapped a bright red scarf around her neck, which had been knitted by Grandma Soozie. She made pleased noises – **HEE HAW, HEE HAW.**

'That will keep you nice and warm,' said Roobie, as she fed her some fresh carrots

which they had brought. She ate them quickly **(almost as quickly as Radley ate his food).** Jeanie was Roobie and Radley's special friend and they **LOVED** her very much.

On the way back up towards Westie Green, they met some of their friends on their way to the party. Archy and Popsie Turner, Miss Tilly Bean and the Winfield Westies, Harvey, Theo and Chloe. They were **EXCITED** to tell them what **SANTA** had brought each of them, and how he had eaten the mince pies and carrots they had left out for the reindeer **(little did they know about Roobie and Radley's little secret).**

When they got back, the **PARTY** had begun with lots of Westie Green Hutters arriving, each wishing each other **MERRY CHRISTMAS.**

Auntie **POPPY** and Mr. Oliver the lock-keeper had made their way up from the canal. They had brought with them empty **jam jars** that had been recycled from the Bones Bakery. Inside were homemade candles made from part-used ones.

Mr. Oliver had made some handles, so they could be hung up in the trees as lanterns. Roobie and Miss Tilly Bean helped to hang them, and they clapped their paws together when they had finished.

'**Oooh,** they look just like **MOONBEAMS** in a jar,' said Roobie.

Sir Wesley arrived in his full **HIGHLAND DRESS** and he had brought his bagpipes with him. He might have been one of the oldest Westies in the community, but he could still blow a good old **bag of wind** when it came to his pipes! Farmer McGruff had also brought his and together they were going to pipe the haggis and Christmas pudding out onto the table. This is **an ancient Scottish tradition** that they continued every Christmas in Westie Green.

The Christmas table was made of several large **LONG** pieces of wood, which were placed on top of **SAWN OFF** tree stumps. The chairs were also stumps. Both had been made from a **TREE** that had been struck by lightning and had fallen down. Everything in Westie Green was reused in some way or the other.

The table was full of all types of Christmas **GOODIES** that you could think of or wish for. All of the Westie Hutters had brought food to share with everyone in their little community.

Roobie and Radley's parents had roasted both a **WOODLAND** mushroom loaf and a **HUGE** turkey with all the trimmings. There were big golden-brown roasted tatties **(potatoes),** neeps **(swede)**, peas, sprouts and carrots, to name but a few.

CRACKERS

Great big jugs of **THICK** vegetable or turkey & cranberry gravy were passed up and down the table, made with the same recipe that the Bones Bakery used on their **TARTAN BONES** biscuits.

All the **YOUNG** Westie Hutters sat together the one end of the table, where they pulled crackers that Mrs. Fluffytastic McLean had made. Inside were coloured paper hats and small **KNITTED** woodland animals.

Radley and Archy had a lovely time **FLICKING** spilled peas on the table at each other, until they were told off by Sir Wesley, who was waiting to pipe the haggis and Christmas **PUDDING** in.

'Aye, you wee young **RASCALS**, I think you need to clean all those peas up and eat at least two sprouts each!' He stood over them both and watched. Archy **HOOVERED** the peas up with his mouth, and then both he and Radley screwed their faces up and **CHEWED** two sprouts each.

Archy's eyes went as round as buttons as he struggled to get the **SPROUTS** down. Radley made a similar face of disgust, but what Sir Wesley didn't know was that he absolutely **LOVED** sprouts, and this was not a punishment for him at all! Radley delighted in his little secret he kept to himself.

Sir Wesley and Farmer McGruff did a grand job piping in first the **haggis** and then the **Christmas Pudding,** which had **BIG** blue and orange flames from the brandy that Mr. Brown had poured over the pudding. Then it was lit and carried it out from the bakery to loud cheers from everybody.

Grandma Soozie stood there looking **PROUDLY** at the pudding she had made. She didn't have to remind Radley to eat it slowly, as he had remembered to look for **HIDDEN TREASURE** and told all his friends they had to do same.

Within moments Radley shouted, with yellow **CUSTARD** all around his whiskers, 'I've found some!' He held his bowl and spoon up in the air and a **small silver coin.**

The rest of the **young** Hutters dug with their spoons and soon there were further shouts of hidden treasure **FINDS!**

There were other delicious desserts and puddings. There were **HOMEMADE** apple and rhubarb pies made by **Mrs. Isla McGruff** from the fruit from their farm. There was lemon and lime fizzy sherbet trifle, which had bright **GREEN JELLY FROGS** set in the bottom, **Scottish** raspberry profiteroles piled up high as a Highland mountain, with McGruff's white, fluffytastic **dairy cream.**

At the top of the table, Radley spotted that someone had made the most wobblish jellies that he had ever seen, which sat on **SANTA** plates. He absolutely loved jelly – it was his **FAVOURITE.**

When he saw the picture of Santa staring back at him from the plates, he thought to himself and wondered about what **SANTA** might be doing right now.

He told himself that he would be with Mrs. Claus and the reindeer, all of them having their Christmas **DINNER** together.

Radley touched the Santa medal he was carrying in the pocket of his **BEST TARTAN** trousers. He knew for certain **that he would always remember his adventure he had shared with Santa.**

Radley suddenly heard a voice say, 'Radley, have you decided what flavour jelly you would like? You have been staring at them for a long time.'

'Aye, I would like some **blackberry and apple** please,' he said, beaming back at his mother as she put some in a dish for him.

Christmas music was played on an **old-fashioned gramophone** which you had to wind up with a handle. It was another great find by Grandpa Angus on his **deliveries.**

With **TWO** bagpipe players, Sir Wesley and Farmer McGruff, they took it in turns to have a rest. There was lots of **TRADITIONAL SCOTTISH** dancing taking place, with Mr. and Mrs. Dalzell dancing the whole of the evening and only stopping briefly for a drink of **mulled wine.**

Grandpa Angus and Grandma Soozie also took to the snowy dance floor along with **Auntie POPPY** who danced with Mr. Oliver and Rufus the Bear until the wee small hours.

Disco and Radley had so much fun dancing together and entertained everybody with their very own version of the **Highland fling!** It had their mother and father and some of the older Westie Hutters saying that they had not **LAUGHED** so much for years.

As night fell, the **MOON** shone down through the snowy branches of the trees like a **spotlight** on a stage of Westie Woods. The hanging jam jar **LANTERNS** gave out a truly magical glow, the coloured fairy lights wound around the higher tree branches reflected onto the glass, beautifully coloured moonbeams. Just like the colours of the **NORTHERN LIGHTS,** thought Roobie. This had to be one of the **MOST** enchanting places to be, she thought, as she stared up at the moon. She had seen some wonderful places in her adventure with Santa, but right now this was the **only place in the WORLD that she wanted to be.**

They had all had such a **WONDERFUL** Christmas day, and they climbed the wooden ladder to their bedroom and snuggled into their warm crocodile beds. Disco was fast **ASLEEP** within seconds, all four of his trotters in the air. All the fresh air, food and dancing had worn him out.

Just before Roobie climbed into bed, she pulled out a small handwritten note that she had **FOUND** tucked in the top of her Christmas STOCKING. She showed Radley. It read,

Always believe in the **MAGIC** *of Christmas and keep that* **MAGIC in** *your heart always.*
Merry Christmas *Roobie, Radley and Disco,*
Love SANTA XX.

'**WOW**, goodness, wasn't that an **AMAZING** adventure we had this Christmas?' said Roobie.

'Aye, I don't think we will ever have **a better one!'** said Radley, yawning.

Just outside their bedroom **THE TREE OF AWESOMENESS** rustled its snowy branches in the moonlight.

Well, we will just have to wait and see…

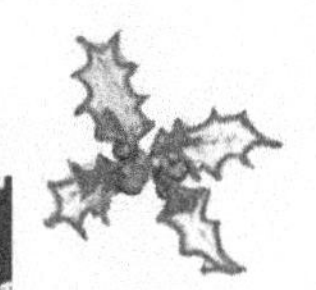

Roobie & Radley with their mummy, author Catherine Brown, visiting Santa

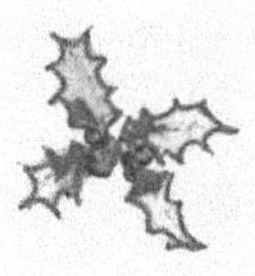

Three more of Catherine's much-loved fluffytastic friends

The Real Westie Green Hutters

The Real Westie Green Hutters

Interesting Facts about the Real Roobie & Radley

ROOBIE'S name is said just the way it is written; **ROO** as in Kangaroo and then **BIE** as in Bee. She is sometimes called Roobie Roo, or Roobs!

Her most favourite things are grabbing hold of the cushions in her mouth from the sofa and **throwing** them on the floor when she sees someone walk past the house. She also loves rolling on her back with her **paws in the air** and often sleeps like this.

RADLEY is often called Master Radley, Radders or sometimes Rascal or **little scallywag!** His most favourite things to do are getting wet, which includes jumping in the bath or shower, **pinching shoes**, emptying bins, and ripping up toilet rolls!

Their best friends are **Archy** and **Popsie Turner**. They often all meet up and go on **shopping trips** to the garden centre with their mummies pushing them in the trolley. They particularly enjoy going down the dog **toy aisle** and choosing their **own** toys!

They have a wooden **Beach Hut** kennel in the garden the exact same colour as the one in the story. They also have a paddling pool and **sand pit**. Roobie only ever gets in the pool for a photo as she **hates** getting wet. However, she can often be found sunning herself on the sand, or as she likes to call it, **the beach!**

They both **love watching TV** and their favourite programme is Countryfile as there are lots of sheep and other **animals** on it.

Going to the **seaside** with their mummy in the summer in their **VW** Campervan called Daisy is, in the words of Radley, **'just Awesome!'**

About the Author and Illustrator

Catherine left school with only a handful of written qualifications. School didn't accommodate or suit her needs as a **DYSLEXIC**. However, if **EFFORT** and **DETERMINATION** had been recognised as achievements then she would have excelled.

Never being prepared to take **'NO'** for an answer, she managed to move from leaving school at 16 as a Hairdresser, to a career spanning more than **two** decades as a **POLICE SERGEANT**. Sadly, her career ended after being injured in the line of her duty leaving her with a permanent **DISABILITY** to her foot.

Looking for a **purpose** and reason to get out of bed each day, she has returned to her childhood love of **ART**. Tapping into her creative talents she has both written and illustrated her **FIRST** children's book, *The Adventures of Roobie & Radley and the Christmas Campervan Rescue*.

She has two **West Highland Terriers** and a **VW CAMPERVAN**, which both provided the idea, and inspiration for her book.

Roobie & Radley added; we think mummy also loves Christmas as we had fourteen trees up the last time we counted!

CAN YOU FIND A WAY DOWN

THE SNOWY HILL TO HELP RADLEY

GET BACK TO GRANDPA ANGUS & ROOBIE?

Lightning Source UK Ltd.
Milton Keynes UK
UKHW051237081119
353142UK00005B/90/P